SKYLANDERS

THE KAOS TRAP

WELCOME TO SKYLANDER ACADEMY

Story by:
RON MARZ and **DAVID A. RODRIGUEZ**

Art by:
FICO OSSIO

Colors by:
LEONARDO & ALICE ITO

Letters by:
DERON BENNETT & TOM B. LONG

Edited by:
DAVID HEDGECOCK

 Spotlight

ABDOPUBLISHING.COM

Reinforced library bound edition published in 2016 by Spotlight,
a division of ABDO, PO Box 398166, Minneapolis, Minnesota 55439.
Spotlight produces high-quality reinforced library bound editions for
schools and libraries. Published by agreement with IDW.

Printed in the United States of America, North Mankato, Minnesota.
042015
092015

THIS BOOK CONTAINS
RECYCLED MATERIALS

LIBRARY OF CONGRESS CATALOGING-IN-PUBLICATION DATA

Marz, Ron, author.
 Welcome to Skylander Academy / writer: Ron Marz and David A. Rodriguez ; artist:
Fico Ossio ; colors: Leonardo & Alice Ito.
    pages cm. -- (Skylanders: the kaos trap)
 Summary: "During a tour of the academy, Kaos removes his disguise and attacks!
Tessa, Cali, and the newly found Flynn rush back to the school. Will they be able to
help the students?"-- Provided by publisher.
 ISBN 978-1-61479-388-5
1. Graphic novels. I. Rodriguez, David A., author. II. Ossio, Fico, illustrator. III. Sky-
landers (Game) IV. Title.
 PZ7.7.M3754Wel 2016
 741.5'973--dc23
                    2015001612

Spotlight

A Division of ABDO
abdopublishing.com

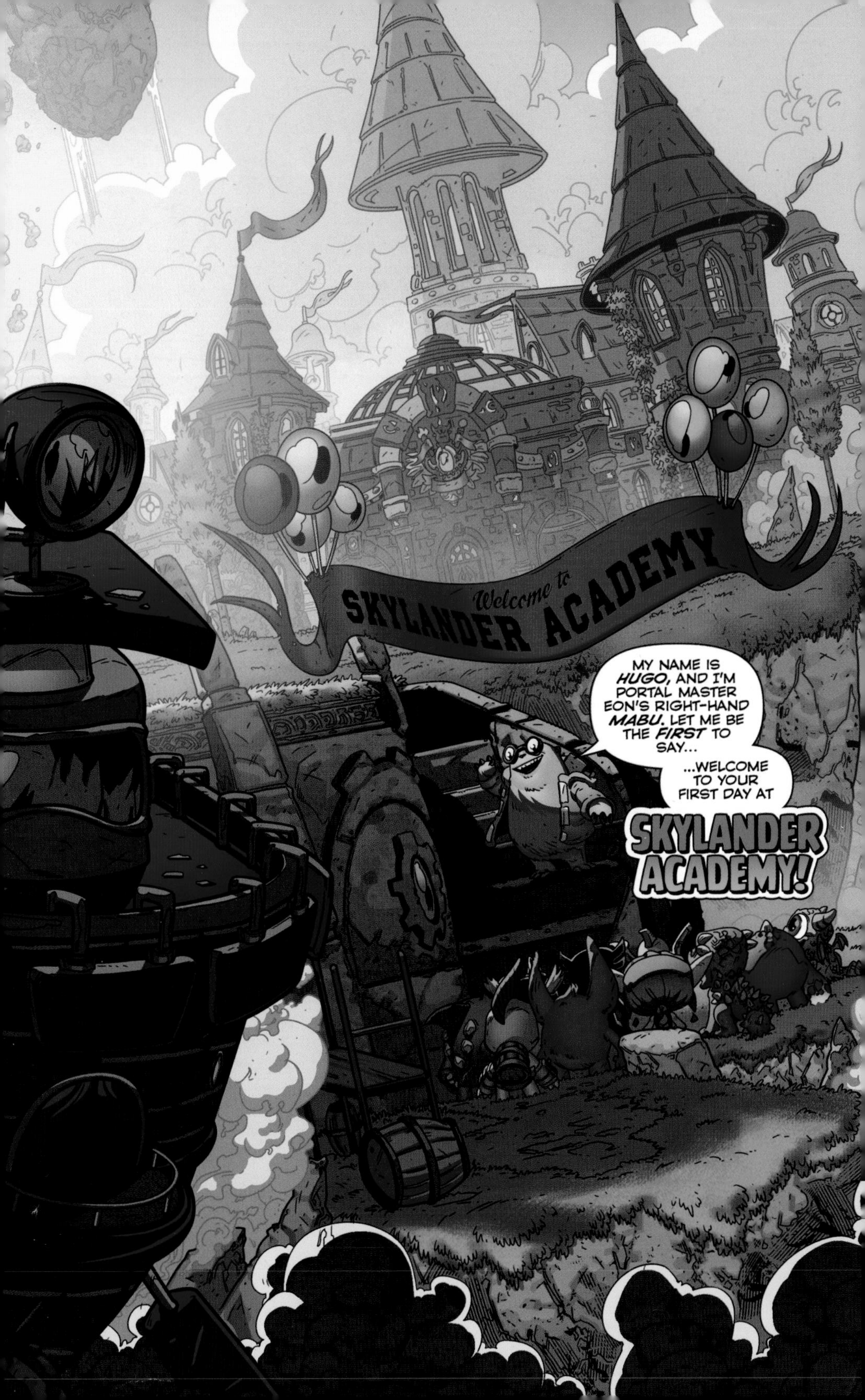
Welcome to
SKYLANDER ACADEMY
MY NAME IS HUGO, AND I'M PORTAL MASTER EON'S RIGHT-HAND MABU. LET ME BE THE FIRST TO SAY...
...WELCOME TO YOUR FIRST DAY AT
SKYLANDER ACADEMY!

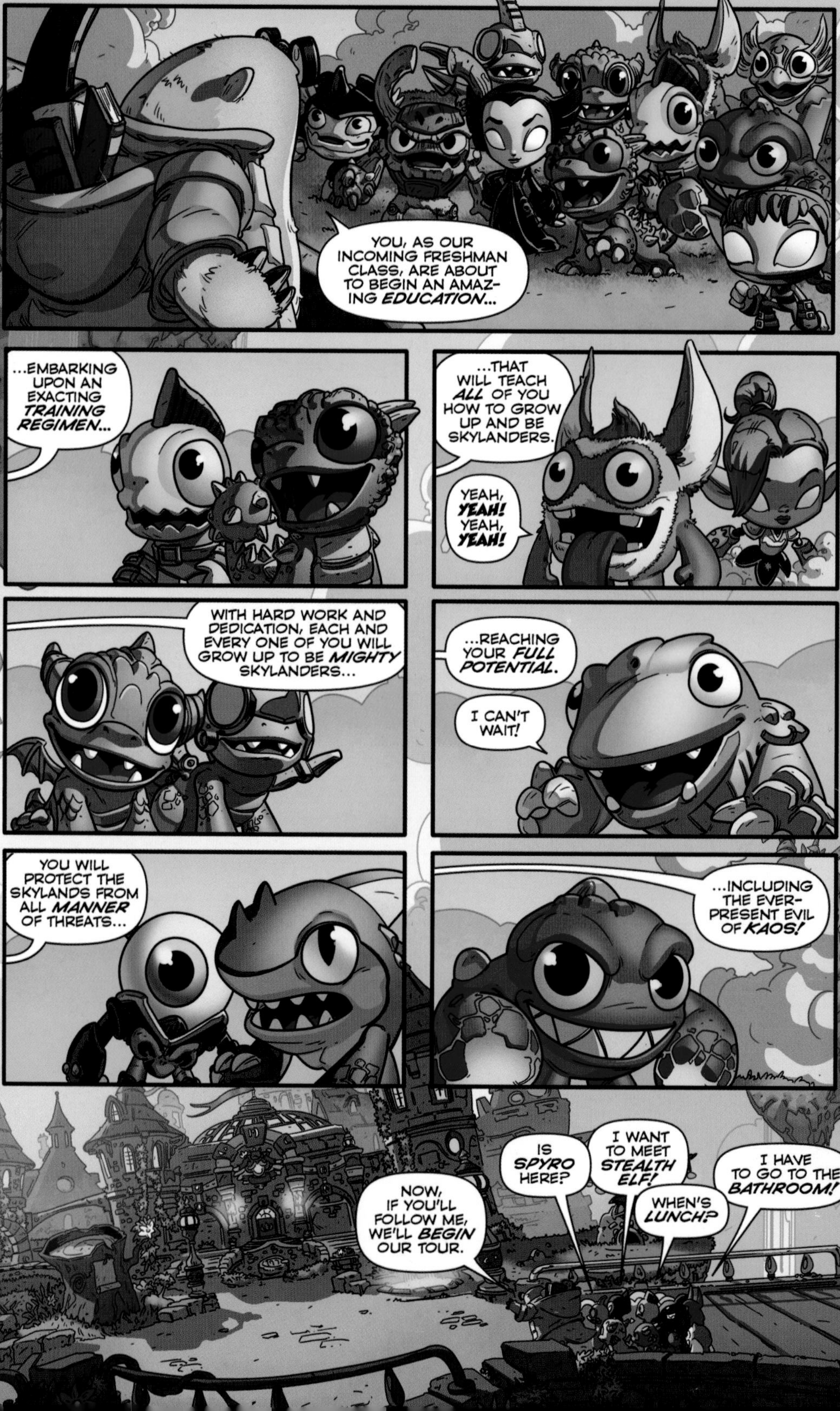
YOU, AS OUR INCOMING FRESHMAN CLASS, ARE ABOUT TO BEGIN AN AMAZ-ING *EDUCATION*...
...EMBARKING UPON AN EXACTING *TRAINING REGIMEN*...
...THAT WILL TEACH *ALL* OF YOU HOW TO GROW UP AND BE SKYLANDERS.
YEAH, **YEAH!** YEAH, **YEAH!**
WITH HARD WORK AND DEDICATION, EACH AND EVERY ONE OF YOU WILL GROW UP TO BE *MIGHTY* SKYLANDERS...
...REACHING YOUR *FULL POTENTIAL*.
I CAN'T WAIT!
YOU WILL PROTECT THE SKYLANDS FROM ALL *MANNER* OF THREATS...
...INCLUDING THE EVER-PRESENT EVIL OF *KAOS!*
NOW, IF YOU'LL FOLLOW ME, WE'LL *BEGIN* OUR TOUR.
IS *SPYRO* HERE?
I WANT TO MEET *STEALTH ELF!*
WHEN'S *LUNCH?*
I HAVE TO GO TO THE *BATHROOM!*

WE'LL START WITH SOMETHING *VERY* SPECIAL. THIS *HUT* YOU SEE BEHIND ME...

...BELONGS TO *PERSEPHONE*. SHE CAN TRANSFORM GOLD INTO PURE MAGIC...

...AND YOU CAN USE MAGIC TO *UPGRADE* YOUR SKYLANDER ABILITIES.

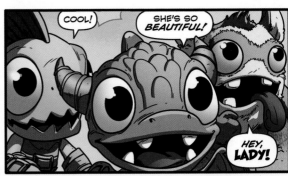

COOL!

SHE'S SO *BEAUTIFUL!*

HEY, LADY!

OVER *HERE*, YOU'LL SEE ONE OF OUR *TRANSPORTER PADS*, WHICH CAN INSTANTLY SEND SKYLANDERS TO LOCATIONS ALL OVER SKYLANDER ACADEMY.

THAT'S *ZOO LOU!*

WELL, THAT *WAS* ZOO LOU.

NOW HE'S PROBABLY OFF ON SOME *EXCITING* ADVENTURE!

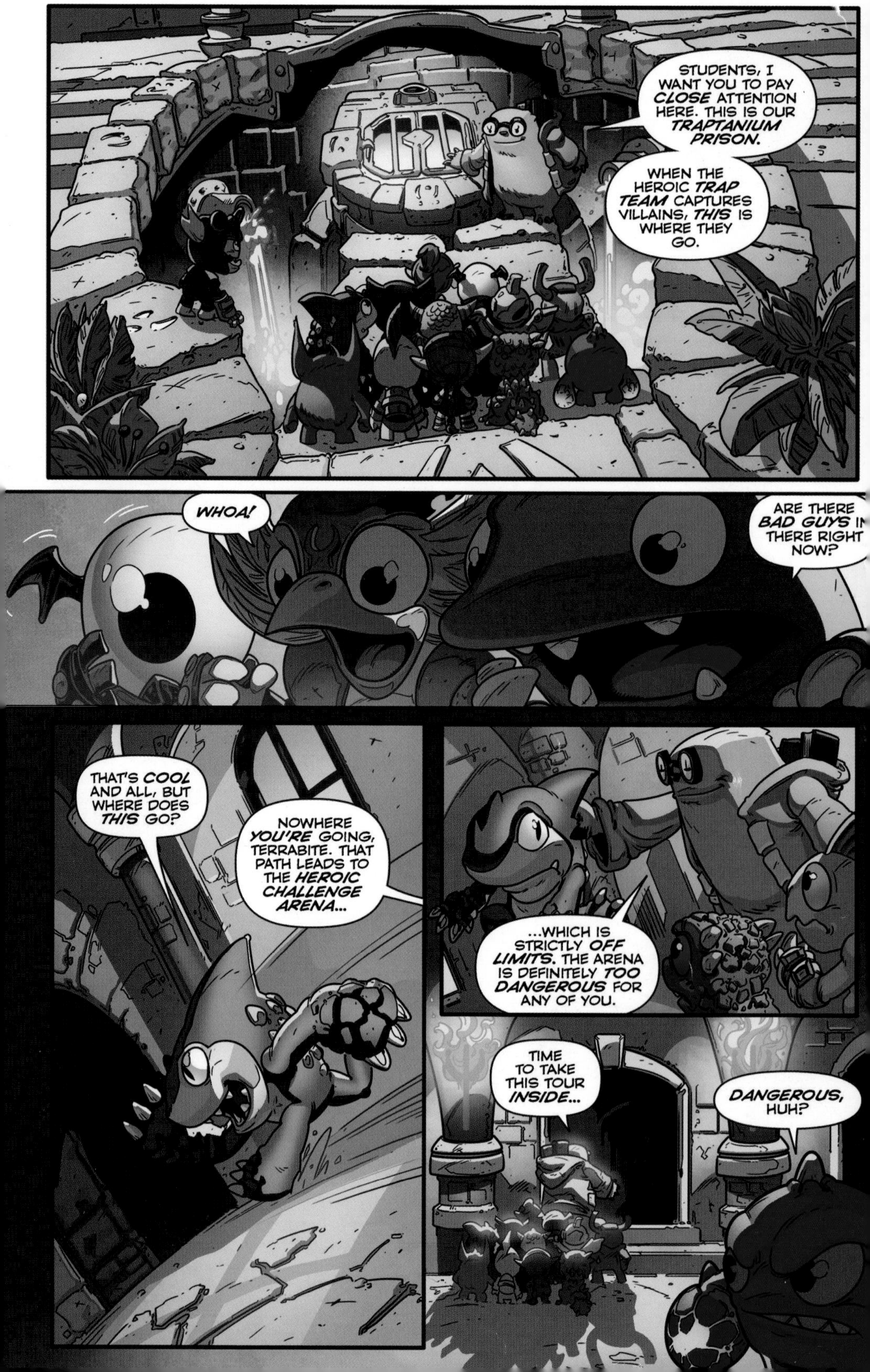
STUDENTS, I WANT YOU TO PAY CLOSE ATTENTION HERE. THIS IS OUR TRAPTANIUM PRISON.
WHEN THE HEROIC TRAP TEAM CAPTURES VILLAINS, THIS IS WHERE THEY GO.
WHOA!
ARE THERE BAD GUYS IN THERE RIGHT NOW?
THAT'S COOL AND ALL, BUT WHERE DOES THIS GO?
NOWHERE YOU'RE GOING, TERRABITE. THAT PATH LEADS TO THE HEROIC CHALLENGE ARENA...
...WHICH IS STRICTLY OFF LIMITS. THE ARENA IS DEFINITELY TOO DANGEROUS FOR ANY OF YOU.
TIME TO TAKE THIS TOUR INSIDE...
DANGEROUS, HUH?

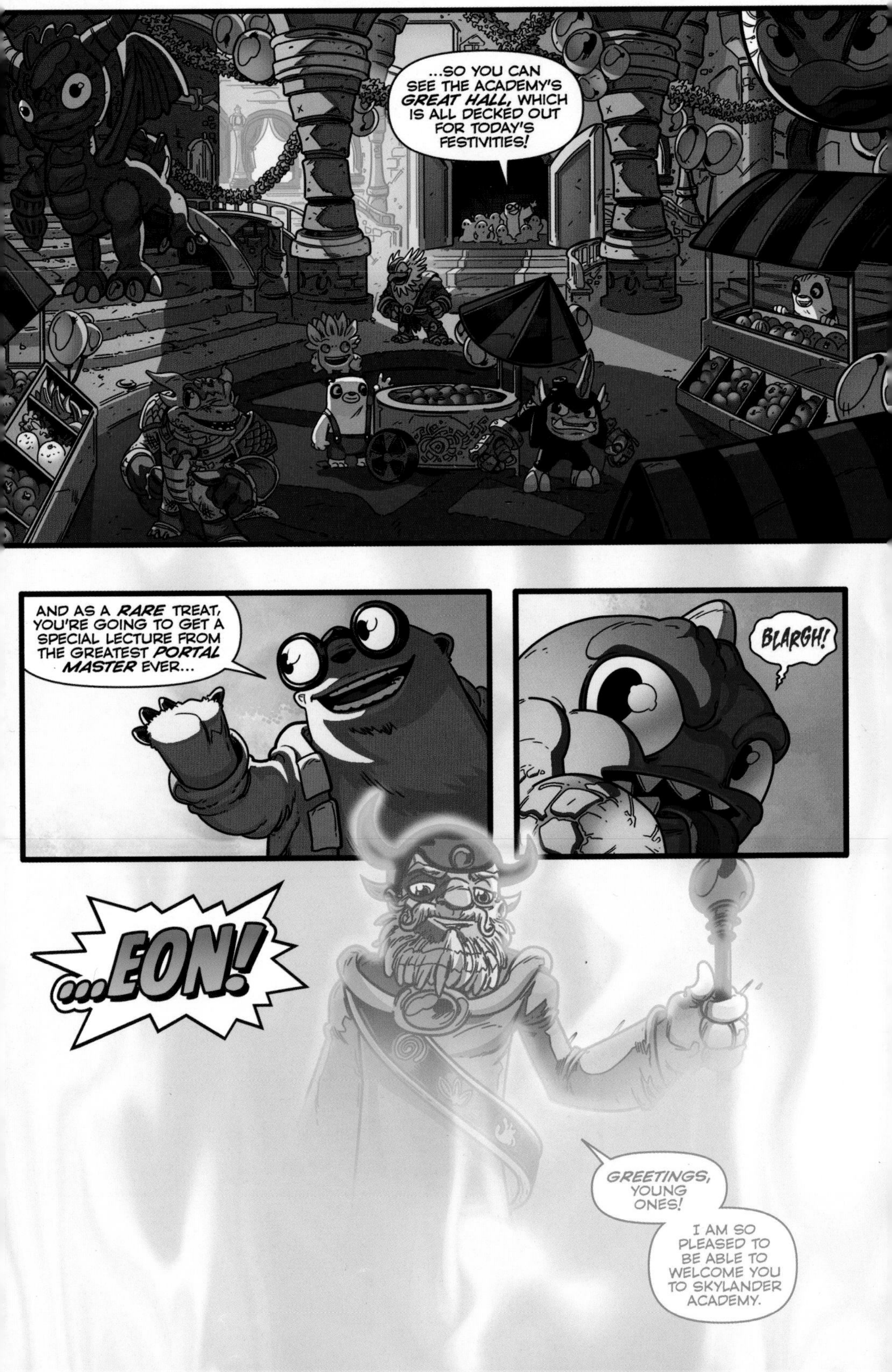
...SO YOU CAN SEE THE ACADEMY'S GREAT HALL, WHICH IS ALL DECKED OUT FOR TODAY'S FESTIVITIES!
AND AS A RARE TREAT, YOU'RE GOING TO GET A SPECIAL LECTURE FROM THE GREATEST PORTAL MASTER EVER...
BLARGH!
...EON!
GREETINGS, YOUNG ONES!
I AM SO PLEASED TO BE ABLE TO WELCOME YOU TO SKYLANDER ACADEMY.

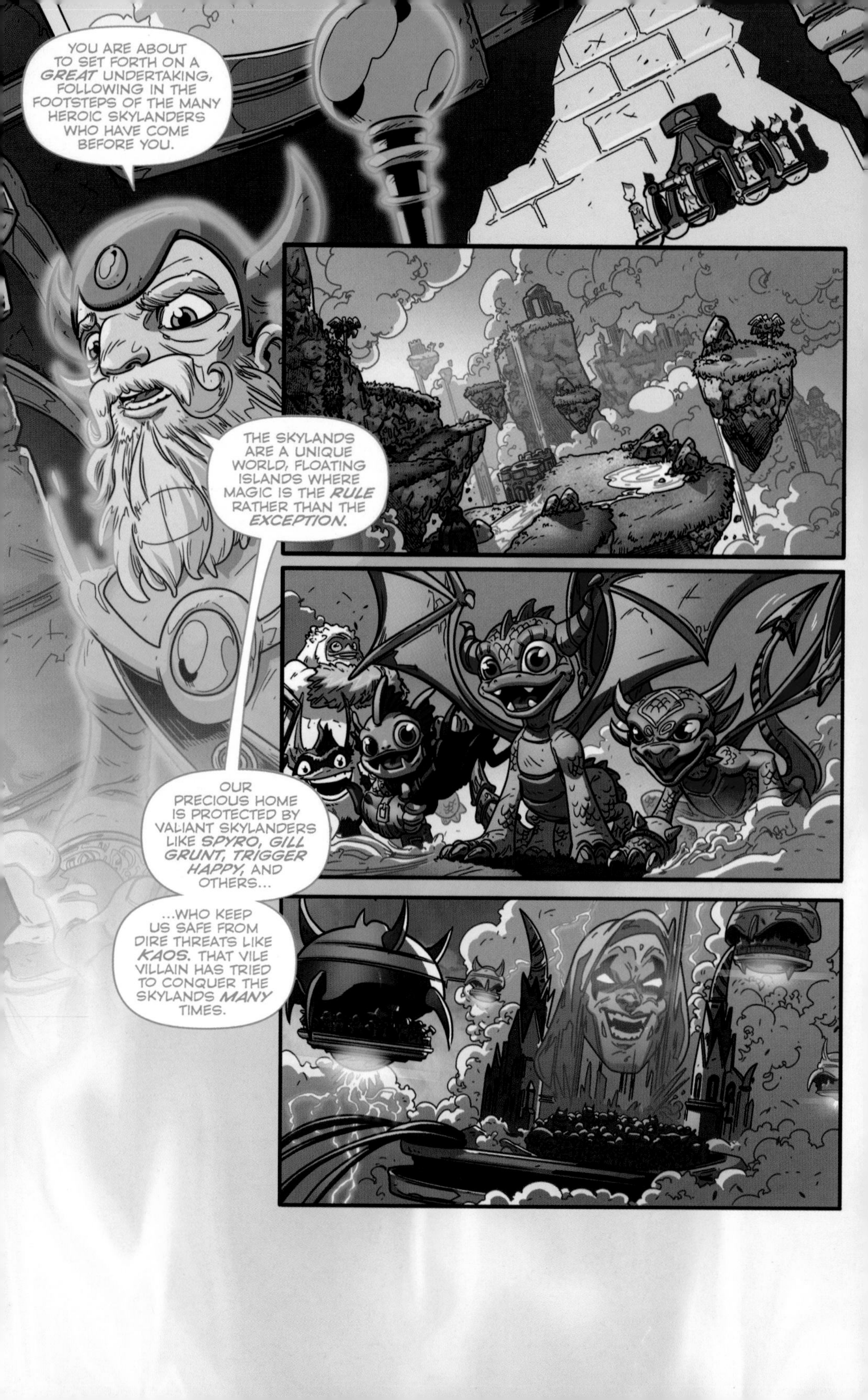
YOU ARE ABOUT TO SET FORTH ON A GREAT UNDERTAKING, FOLLOWING IN THE FOOTSTEPS OF THE MANY HEROIC SKYLANDERS WHO HAVE COME BEFORE YOU.
THE SKYLANDS ARE A UNIQUE WORLD, FLOATING ISLANDS WHERE MAGIC IS THE RULE RATHER THAN THE EXCEPTION.
OUR PRECIOUS HOME IS PROTECTED BY VALIANT SKYLANDERS LIKE SPYRO, GILL GRUNT, TRIGGER HAPPY, AND OTHERS...
...WHO KEEP US SAFE FROM DIRE THREATS LIKE KAOS. THAT VILE VILLAIN HAS TRIED TO CONQUER THE SKYLANDS MANY TIMES.

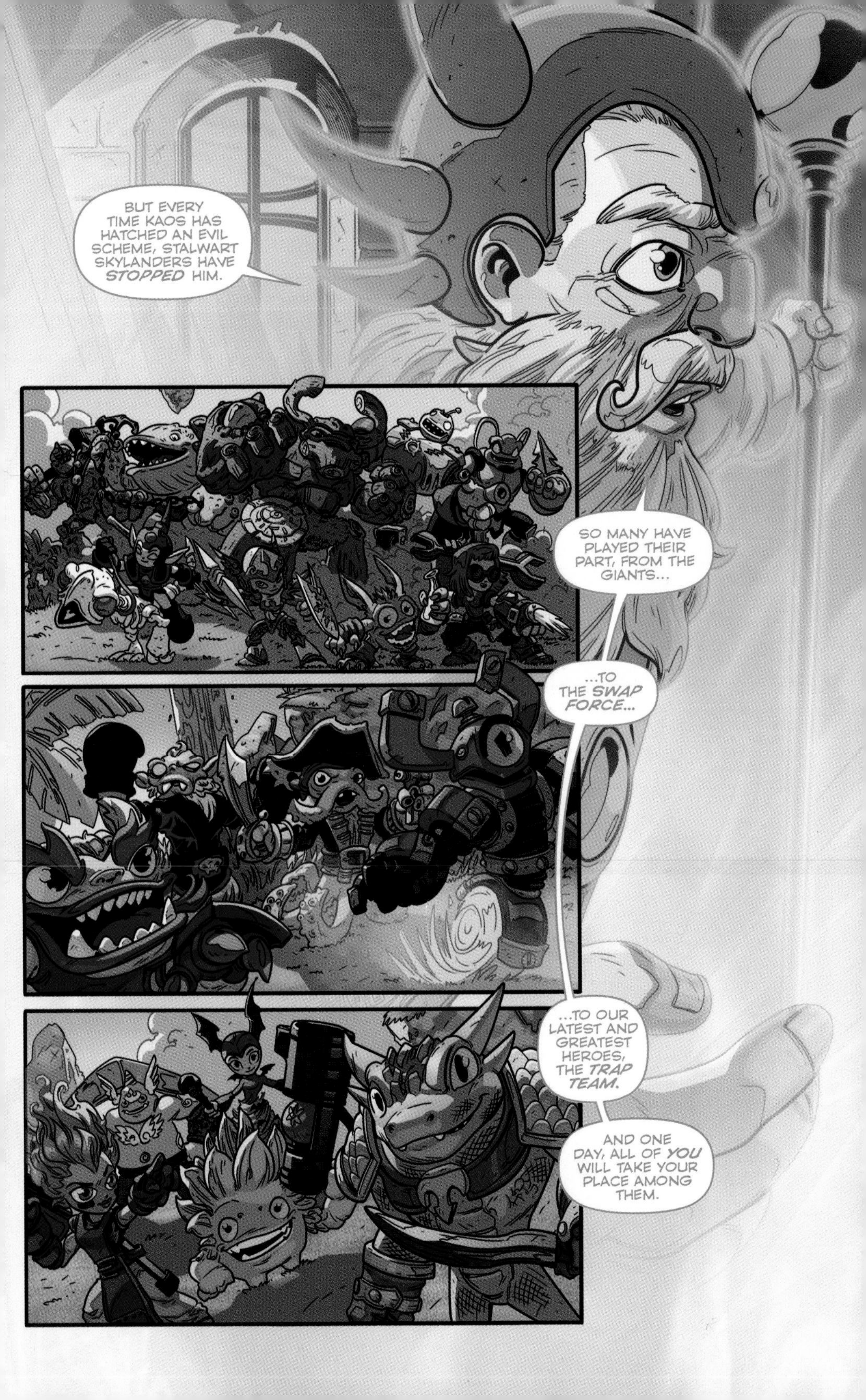
BUT EVERY TIME KAOS HAS HATCHED AN EVIL SCHEME, STALWART SKYLANDERS HAVE *STOPPED* HIM.
SO MANY HAVE PLAYED THEIR PART, FROM THE GIANTS...
...TO THE *SWAP FORCE*...
...TO OUR LATEST AND GREATEST HEROES, THE *TRAP TEAM*.
AND ONE DAY, ALL OF *YOU* WILL TAKE YOUR PLACE AMONG THEM.

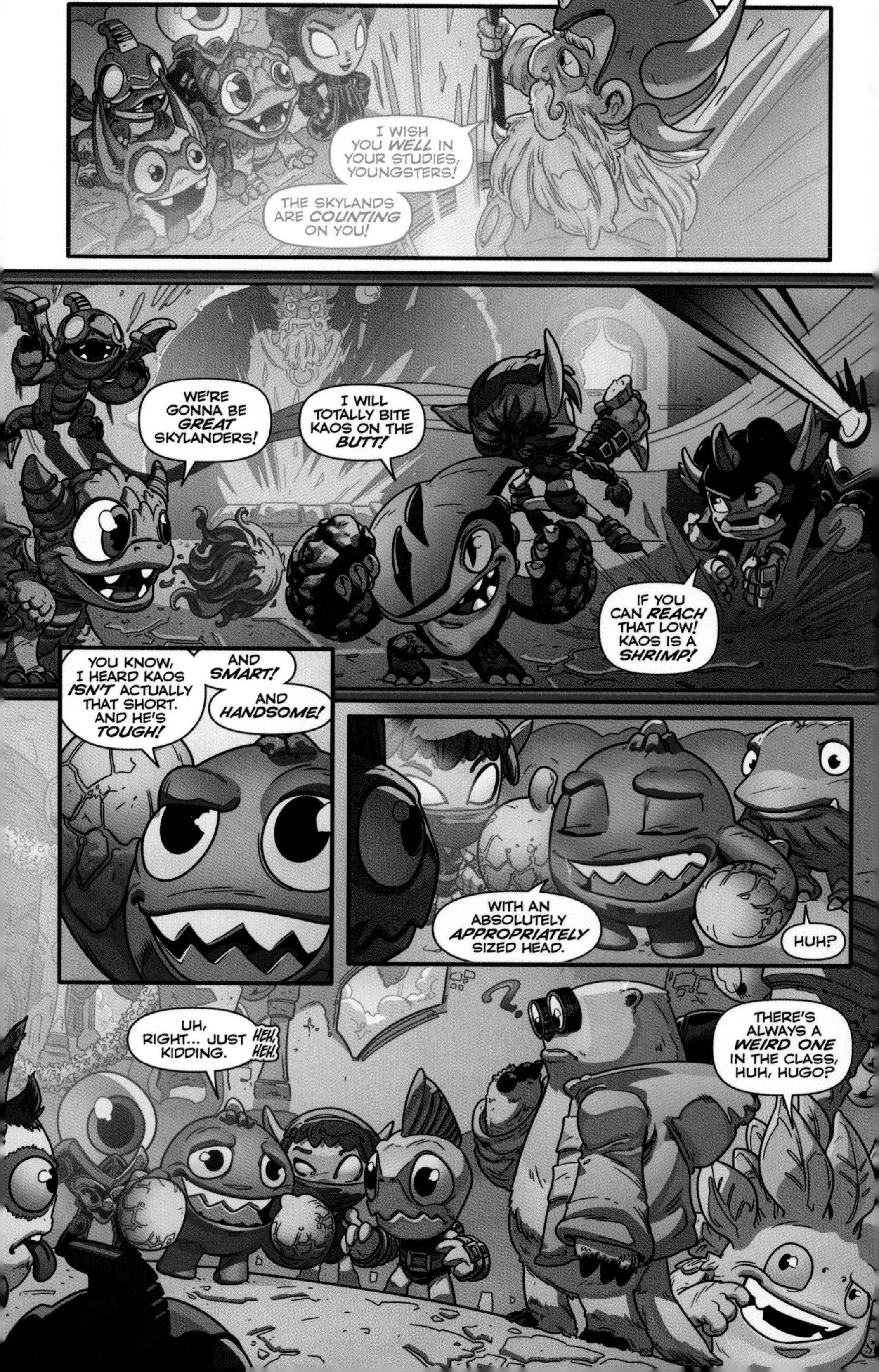
I WISH YOU WELL IN YOUR STUDIES, YOUNGSTERS!
THE SKYLANDS ARE COUNTING ON YOU!
WE'RE GONNA BE GREAT SKYLANDERS!
I WILL TOTALLY BITE KAOS ON THE BUTT!
IF YOU CAN REACH THAT LOW! KAOS IS A SHRIMP!
YOU KNOW, I HEARD KAOS ISN'T ACTUALLY THAT SHORT. AND HE'S TOUGH!
AND SMART!
AND HANDSOME!
WITH AN ABSOLUTELY APPROPRIATELY SIZED HEAD.
HUH?
UH, RIGHT... JUST KIDDING.
HEH, HEH.
THERE'S ALWAYS A WEIRD ONE IN THE CLASS, HUH, HUGO?

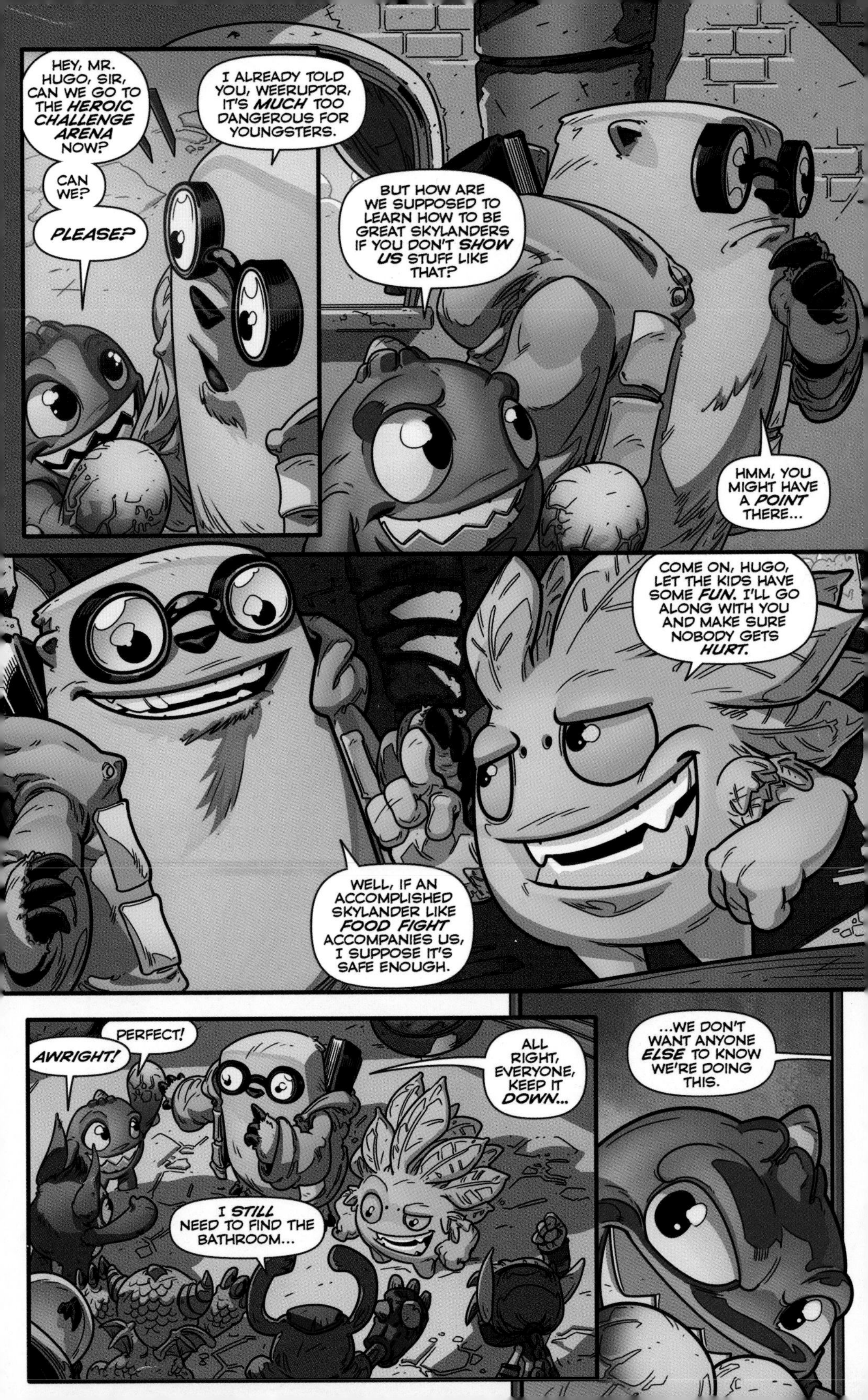
HEY, MR. HUGO, SIR, CAN WE GO TO THE HEROIC CHALLENGE ARENA NOW?
CAN WE?
PLEASE?
I ALREADY TOLD YOU, WEERUPTOR, IT'S MUCH TOO DANGEROUS FOR YOUNGSTERS.
BUT HOW ARE WE SUPPOSED TO LEARN HOW TO BE GREAT SKYLANDERS IF YOU DON'T SHOW US STUFF LIKE THAT?
HMM, YOU MIGHT HAVE A POINT THERE...
COME ON, HUGO, LET THE KIDS HAVE SOME FUN. I'LL GO ALONG WITH YOU AND MAKE SURE NOBODY GETS HURT.
WELL, IF AN ACCOMPLISHED SKYLANDER LIKE FOOD FIGHT ACCOMPANIES US, I SUPPOSE IT'S SAFE ENOUGH.
AWRIGHT!
PERFECT!
ALL RIGHT, EVERYONE, KEEP IT DOWN...
I STILL NEED TO FIND THE BATHROOM...
...WE DON'T WANT ANYONE ELSE TO KNOW WE'RE DOING THIS.

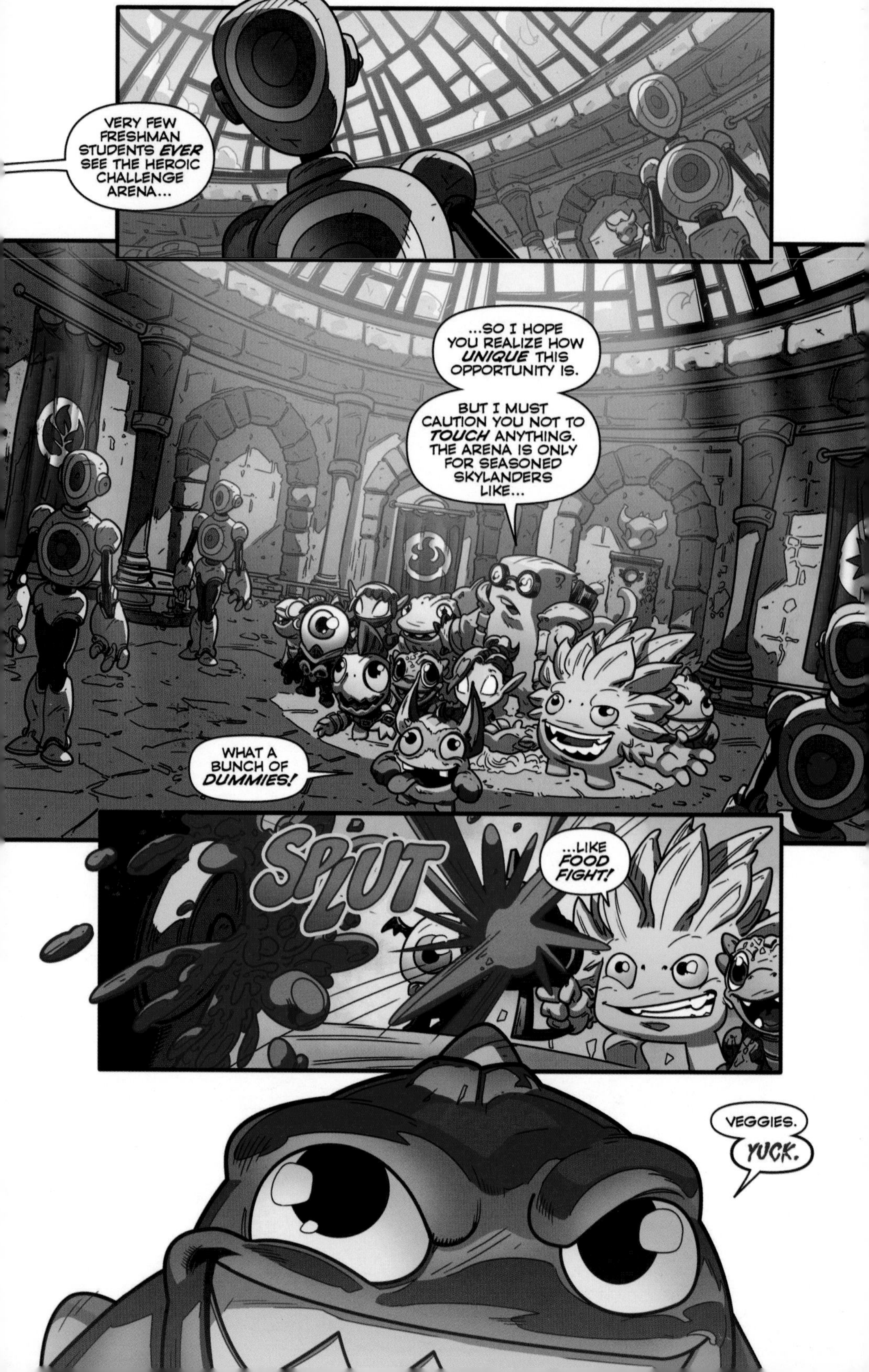

VERY FEW FRESHMAN STUDENTS EVER SEE THE HEROIC CHALLENGE ARENA...
...SO I HOPE YOU REALIZE HOW UNIQUE THIS OPPORTUNITY IS.
BUT I MUST CAUTION YOU NOT TO TOUCH ANYTHING. THE ARENA IS ONLY FOR SEASONED SKYLANDERS LIKE...
WHAT A BUNCH OF DUMMIES!
SPLUT
...LIKE FOOD FIGHT!
VEGGIES.
YUCK.

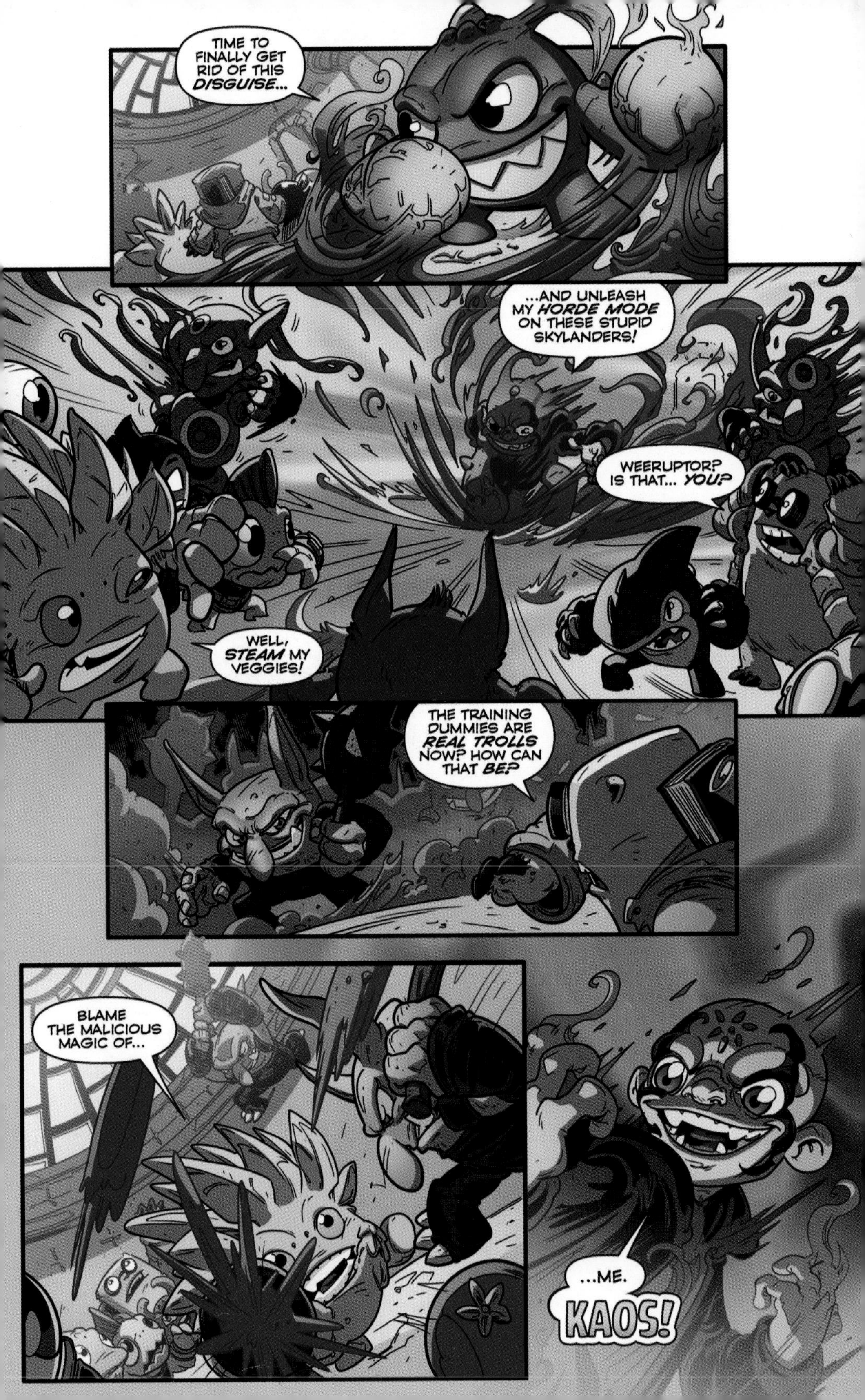
TIME TO FINALLY GET RID OF THIS DISGUISE...
...AND UNLEASH MY HORDE MODE ON THESE STUPID SKYLANDERS!
WEERUPTOR? IS THAT... YOU?
WELL, STEAM MY VEGGIES!
THE TRAINING DUMMIES ARE REAL TROLLS NOW? HOW CAN THAT BE?
BLAME THE MALICIOUS MAGIC OF...
...ME.
KAOS!

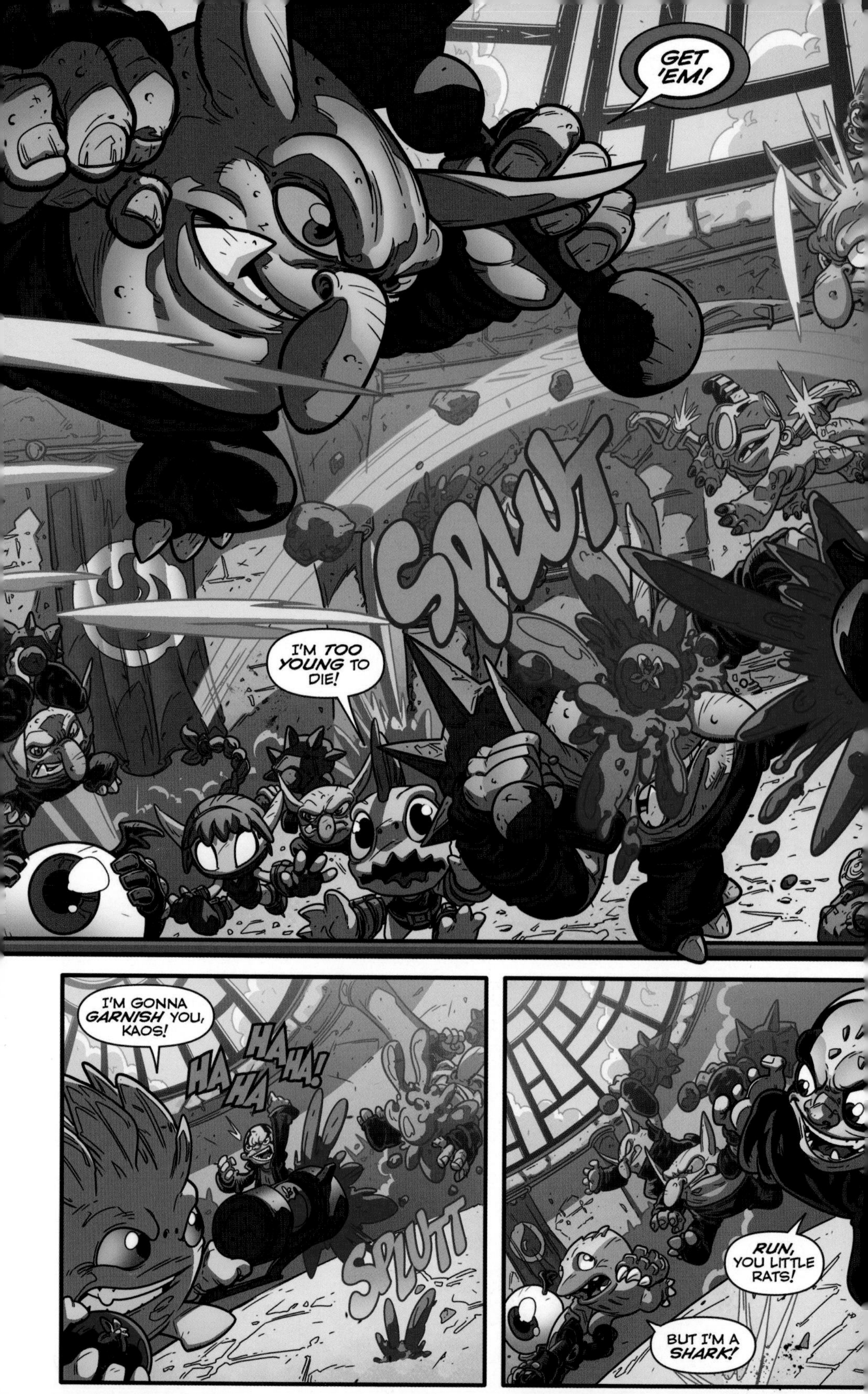
GET 'EM!
SPLUT
I'M *TOO YOUNG* TO DIE!
I'M GONNA *GARNISH* YOU, KAOS!
HA HA HAHA!
SPLUTT
RUN, YOU LITTLE RATS!
BUT I'M A *SHARK!*

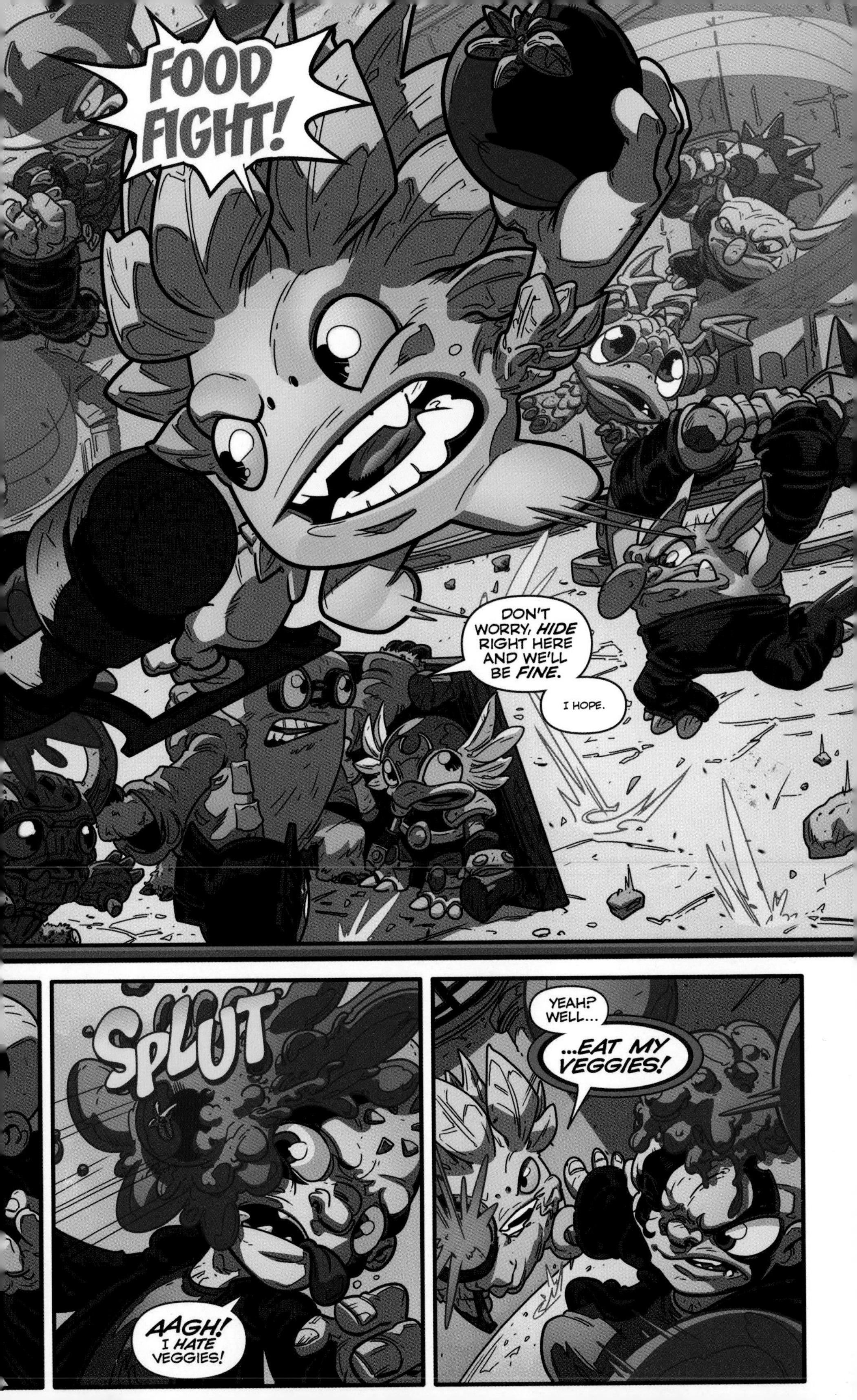
FOOD FIGHT!
DON'T WORRY, *HIDE* RIGHT HERE AND WE'LL BE *FINE*.
I HOPE.
SPLUT
AAGH! I *HATE* VEGGIES!
YEAH? WELL...
...EAT MY VEGGIES!

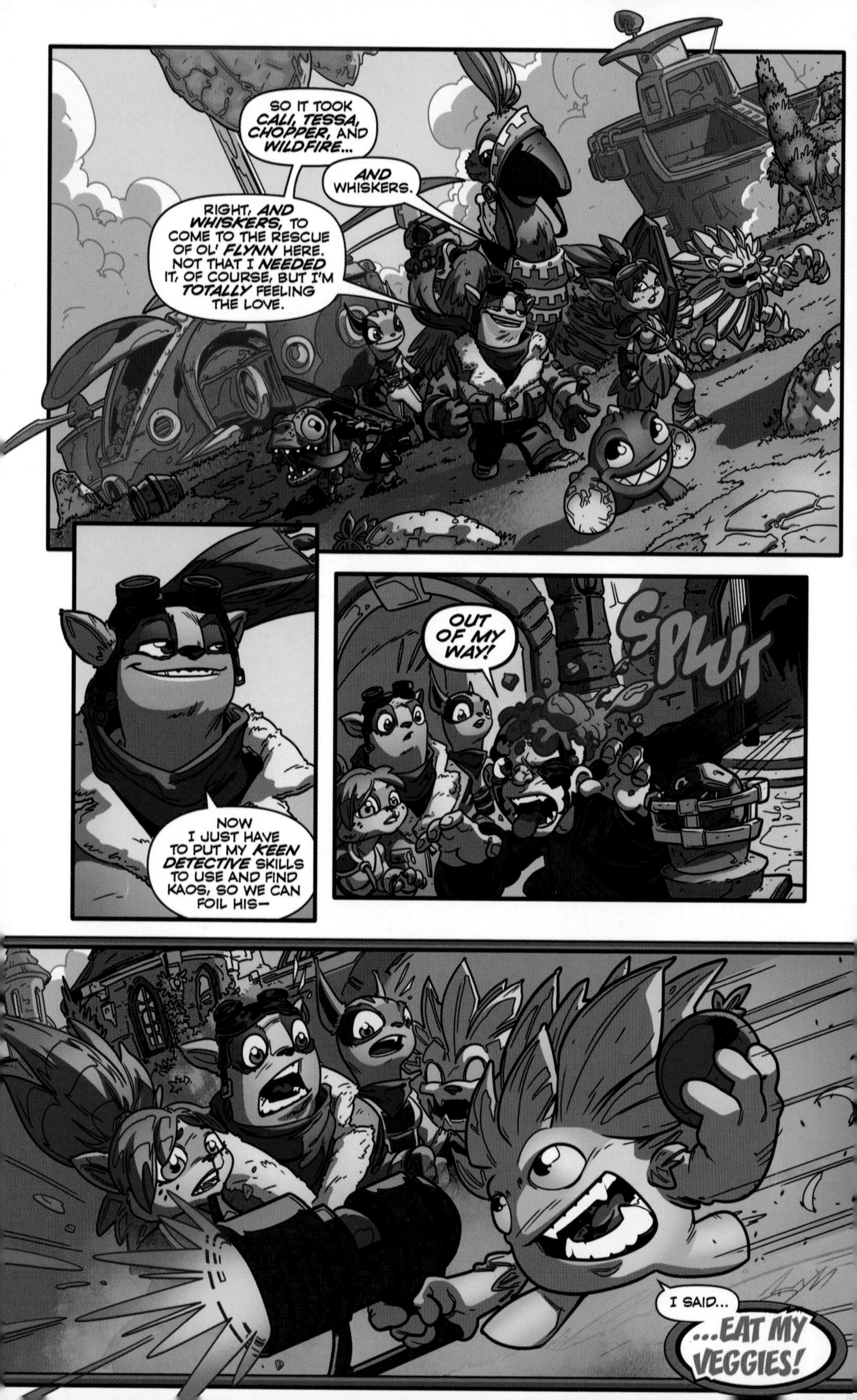
SO IT TOOK CALI, TESSA, CHOPPER, AND WILDFIRE...
AND WHISKERS.
RIGHT, AND WHISKERS, TO COME TO THE RESCUE OF OL' FLYNN HERE. NOT THAT I NEEDED IT, OF COURSE, BUT I'M TOTALLY FEELING THE LOVE.
NOW I JUST HAVE TO PUT MY KEEN DETECTIVE SKILLS TO USE AND FIND KAOS, SO WE CAN FOIL HIS—
OUT OF MY WAY!
SPLUT
I SAID...
...EAT MY VEGGIES!

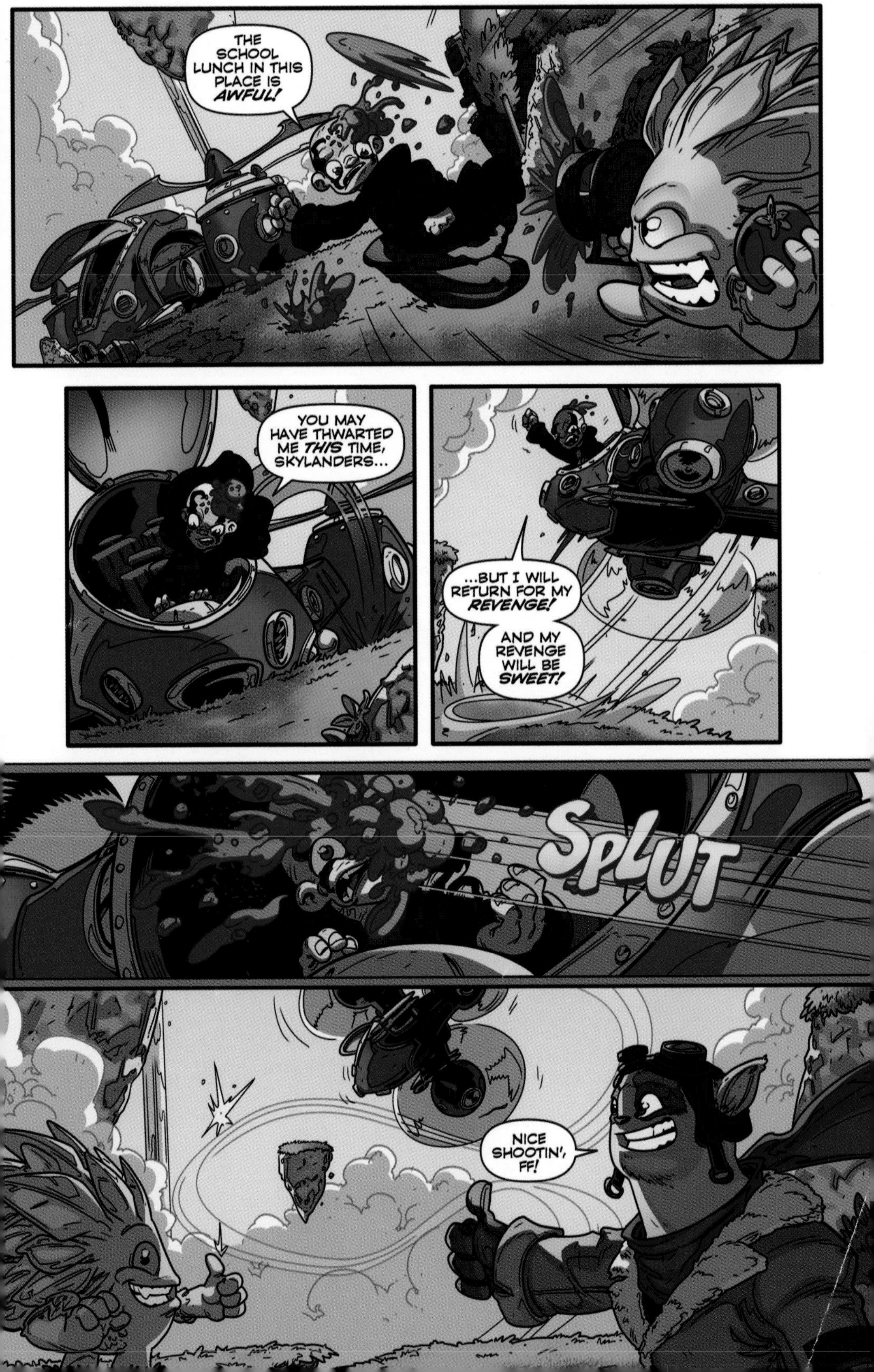
THE SCHOOL LUNCH IN THIS PLACE IS AWFUL!
YOU MAY HAVE THWARTED ME THIS TIME, SKYLANDERS...
...BUT I WILL RETURN FOR MY REVENGE!
AND MY REVENGE WILL BE SWEET!
SPLUT
NICE SHOOTIN', FF!

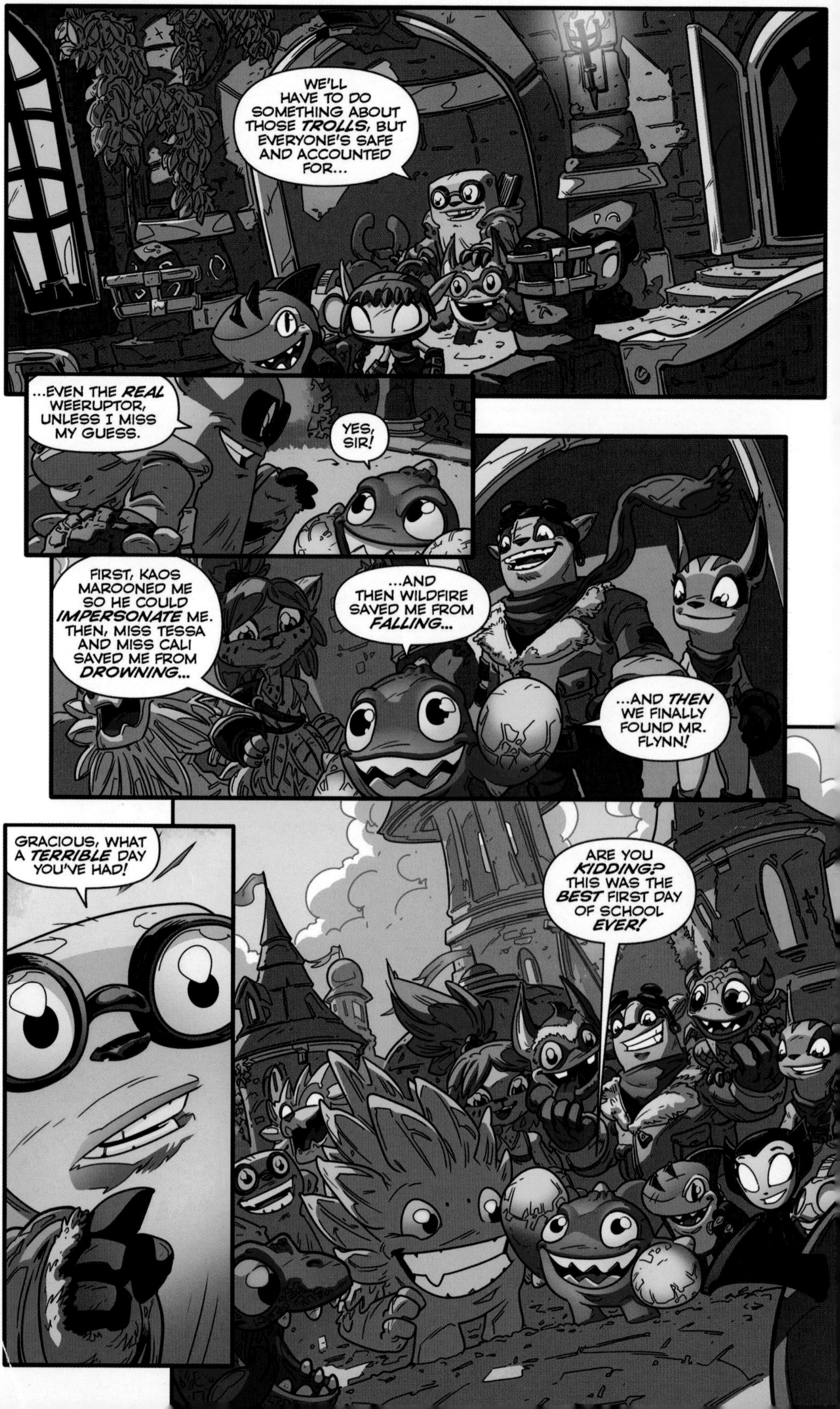

WE'LL HAVE TO DO SOMETHING ABOUT THOSE TROLLS, BUT EVERYONE'S SAFE AND ACCOUNTED FOR...
...EVEN THE REAL WEERUPTOR, UNLESS I MISS MY GUESS.
YES, SIR!
FIRST, KAOS MAROONED ME SO HE COULD IMPERSONATE ME. THEN, MISS TESSA AND MISS CALI SAVED ME FROM DROWNING...
...AND THEN WILDFIRE SAVED ME FROM FALLING...
...AND THEN WE FINALLY FOUND MR. FLYNN!
GRACIOUS, WHAT A TERRIBLE DAY YOU'VE HAD!
ARE YOU KIDDING? THIS WAS THE BEST FIRST DAY OF SCHOOL EVER!

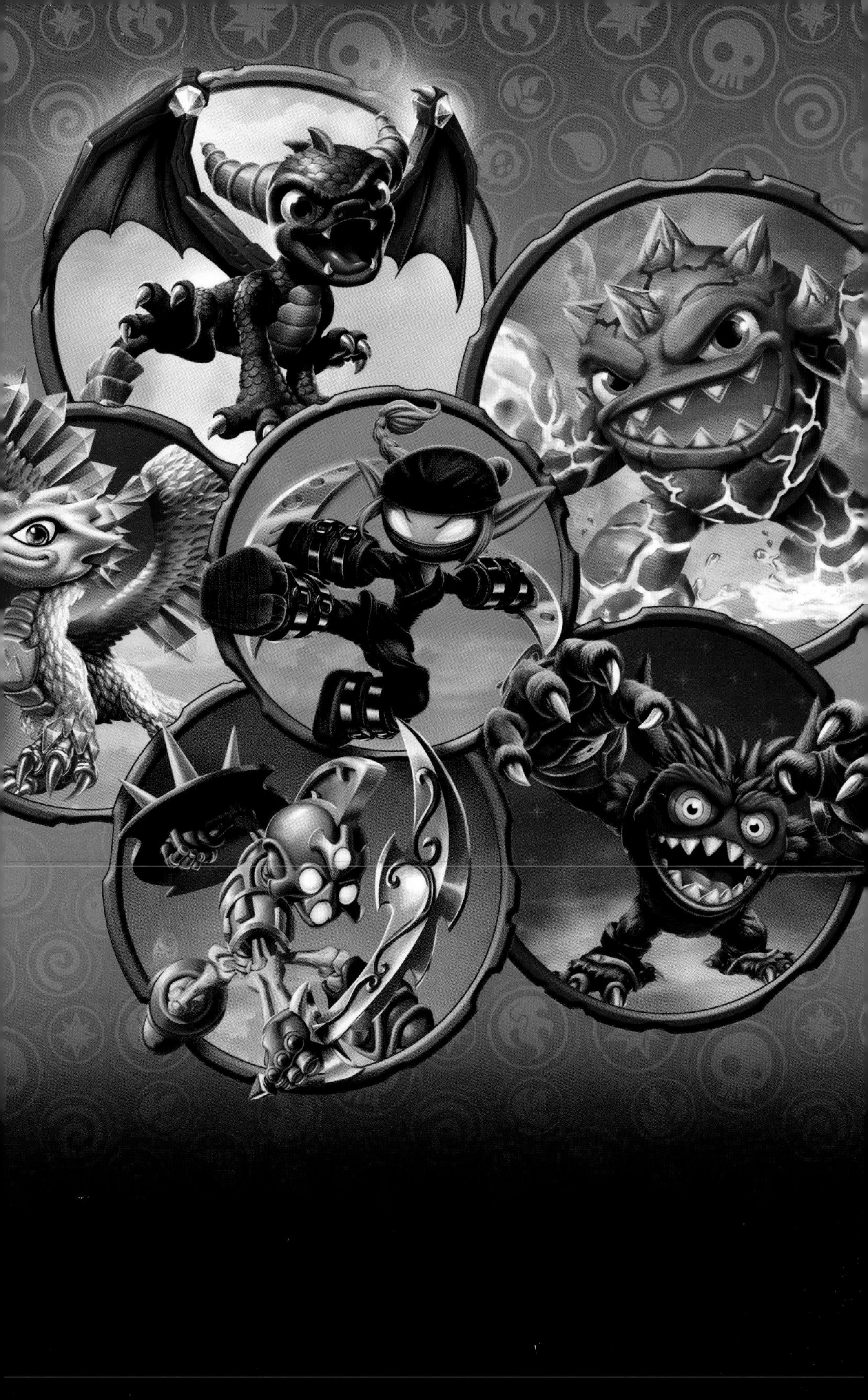

FOOD FIGHT

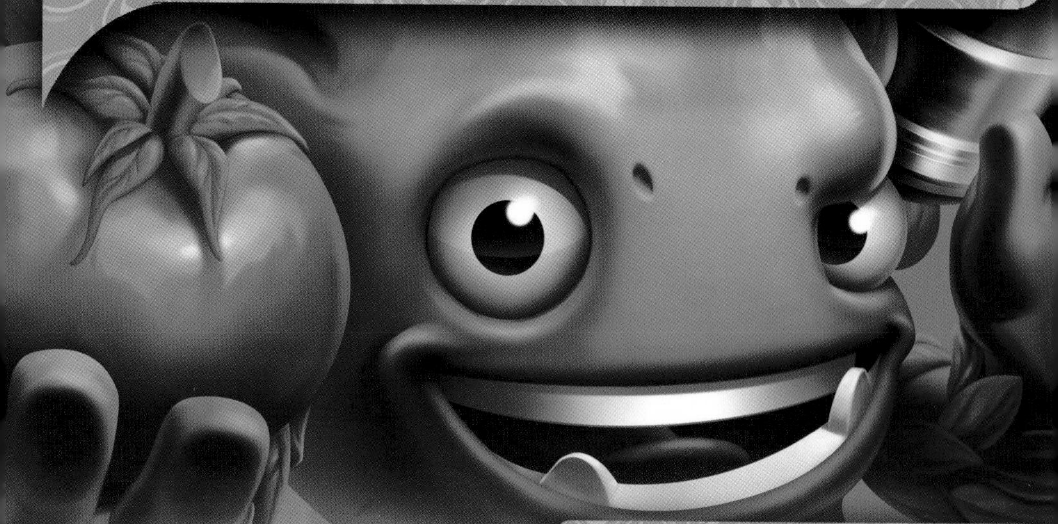

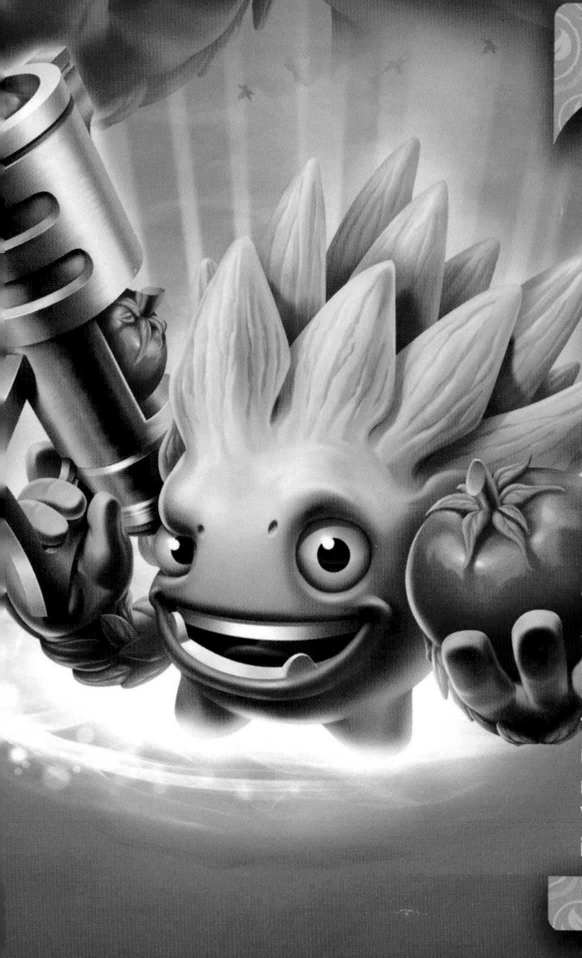

BIO

Food Fight does more than just play with his food, he battles with it! This tough little Veggie Warrior is the byproduct of a troll food experiment gone wrong. When the Troll Farmers Guild attempted to fertilize their soil with gunpowder, they got more than a super snack—they got an all-out Food Fight! Rising from the ground, he led the neighborhood Garden Patrol to victory. Later, he went on to defend his garden home against a rogue army of gnomes after they attempted to wrap the Asparagus people in bacon! His courage caught the eye of Master Eon, who decided that this was one veggie lover he needed on his side as a valued member of the Skylanders. When it comes to Food Fight, it's all you can eat for evil!

WILDFIRE

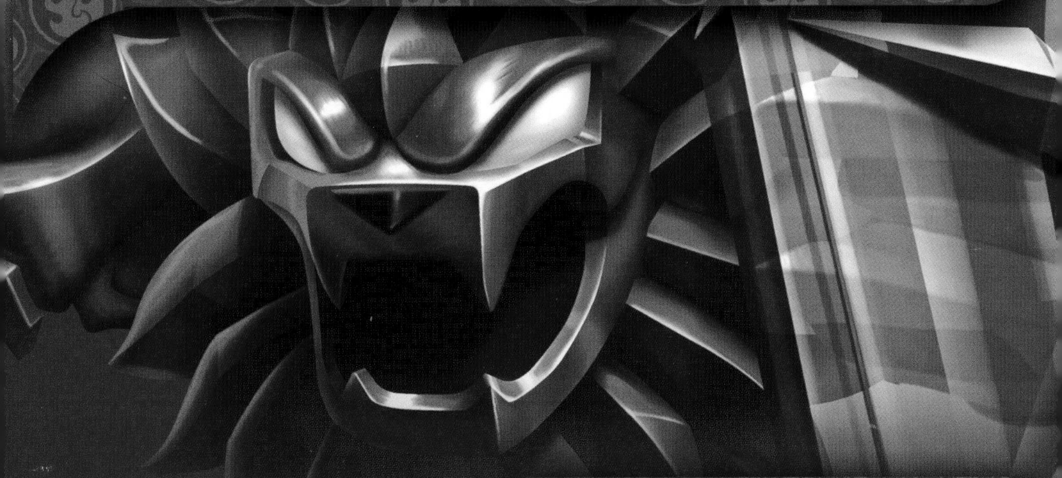

BIO

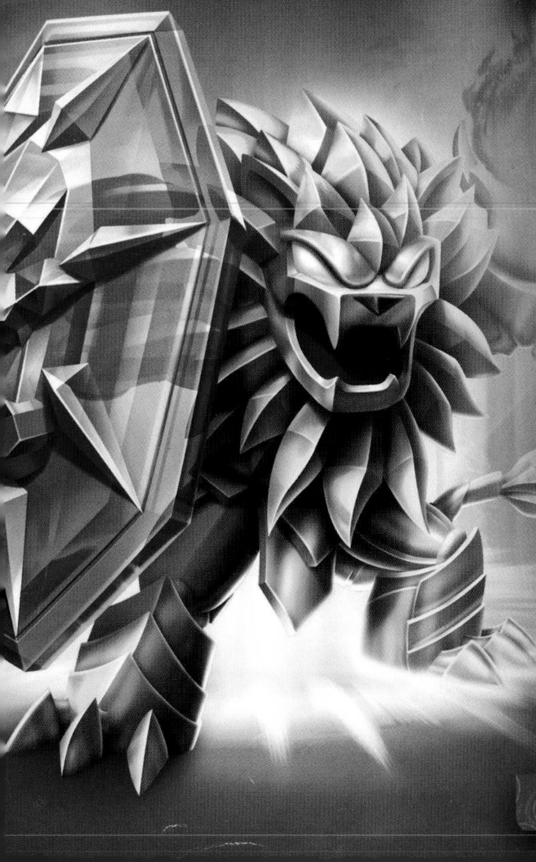

Wildfire was once a young lion of the Fire Claw Clan, about to enter into the Rite of Infernos—a test of survival in the treacherous fire plains. However, because he was made of gold, he was treated as an outcast and not allowed to participate. But this didn't stop him. That night, Wildfire secretly followed the path of the other lions, carrying only his father's enchanted shield. Soon he found them cornered by a giant flame scorpion. Using the shield, he protected the group from the beast's enormous stinging tail, giving them time to safely escape. And though Wildfire was injured in the fight, his father's shield magically changed him—magnifying the strength that was already in his heart—making him the mightiest of his clan. Now part of the Trap Team, Wildfire uses his enormous Traptanium-bonded shield to defend any and all who need it!

SNAP SHOT

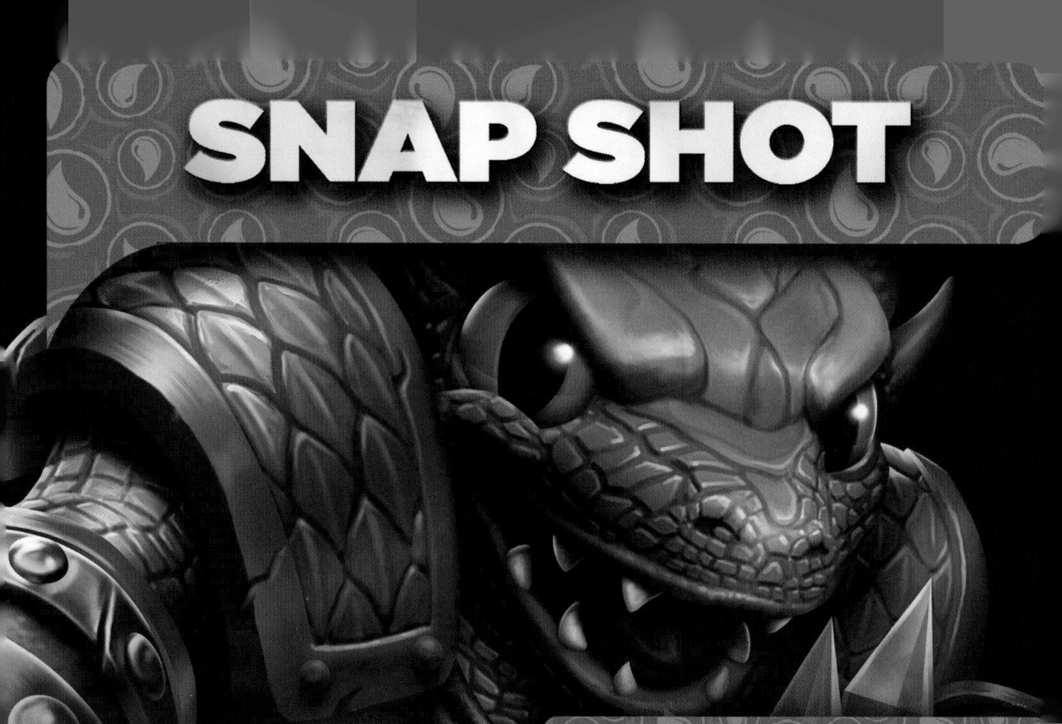

BIO

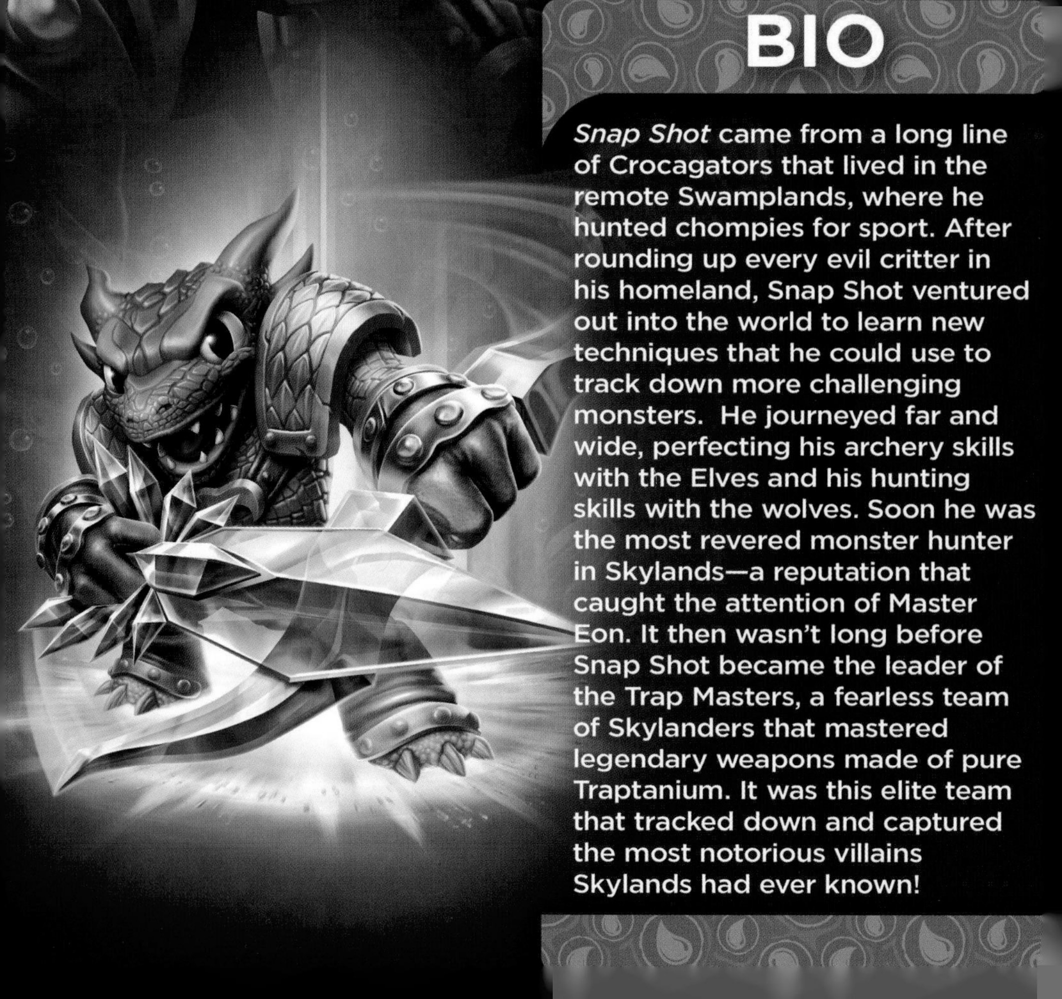

Snap Shot came from a long line of Crocagators that lived in the remote Swamplands, where he hunted chompies for sport. After rounding up every evil critter in his homeland, Snap Shot ventured out into the world to learn new techniques that he could use to track down more challenging monsters. He journeyed far and wide, perfecting his archery skills with the Elves and his hunting skills with the wolves. Soon he was the most revered monster hunter in Skylands—a reputation that caught the attention of Master Eon. It then wasn't long before Snap Shot became the leader of the Trap Masters, a fearless team of Skylanders that mastered legendary weapons made of pure Traptanium. It was this elite team that tracked down and captured the most notorious villains Skylands had ever known!

WALLOP

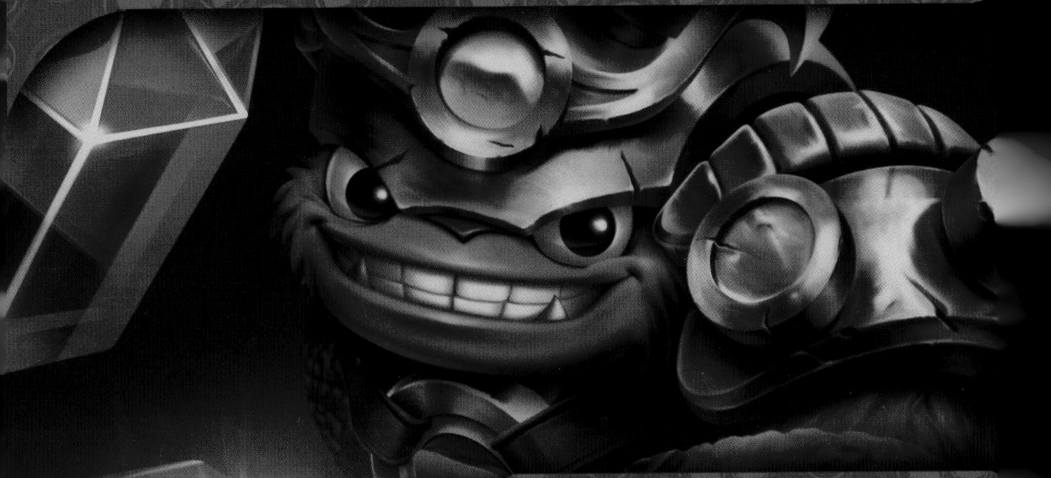

BIO

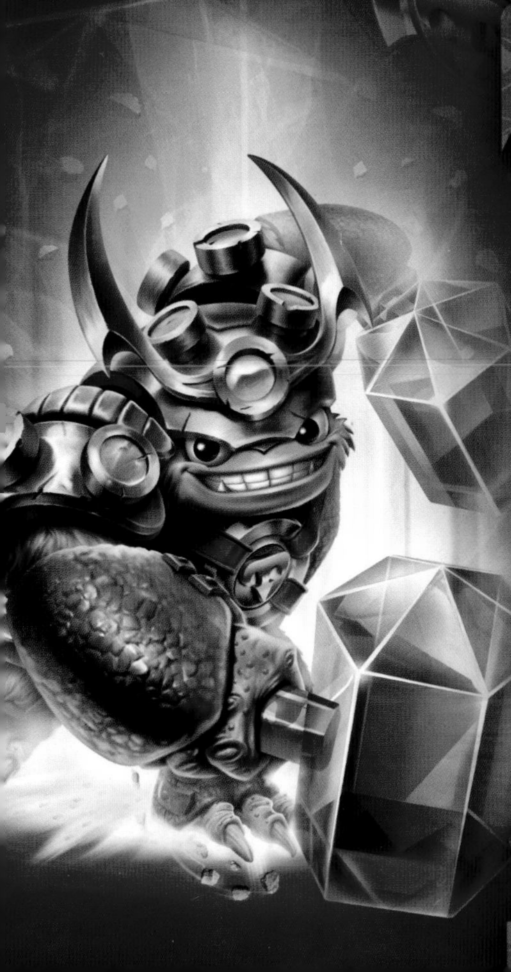

For generations, *Wallop's* people used the volcanic lava pits of Mount Scorch to forge the most awesome weapons in all of Skylands. And Wallop was the finest apprentice any of the masters had ever seen. Using hammers in both of his mighty hands, he could tirelessly pound and shape the incredibly hot metal into the sharpest swords or the hardest axes. But on the day he was to demonstrate his skills to the masters of his craft, a fierce fire viper awoke from his deep sleep in the belly of the volcano. The huge snake erupted forth, attacking Wallop's village. But by bravely charging the beast with his two massive hammers, Wallop was able to bring down the creature and save his village. Now with his Traptanium-infused hammers, he fights with the Skylanders to protect the lands from any evil that rises to attack!

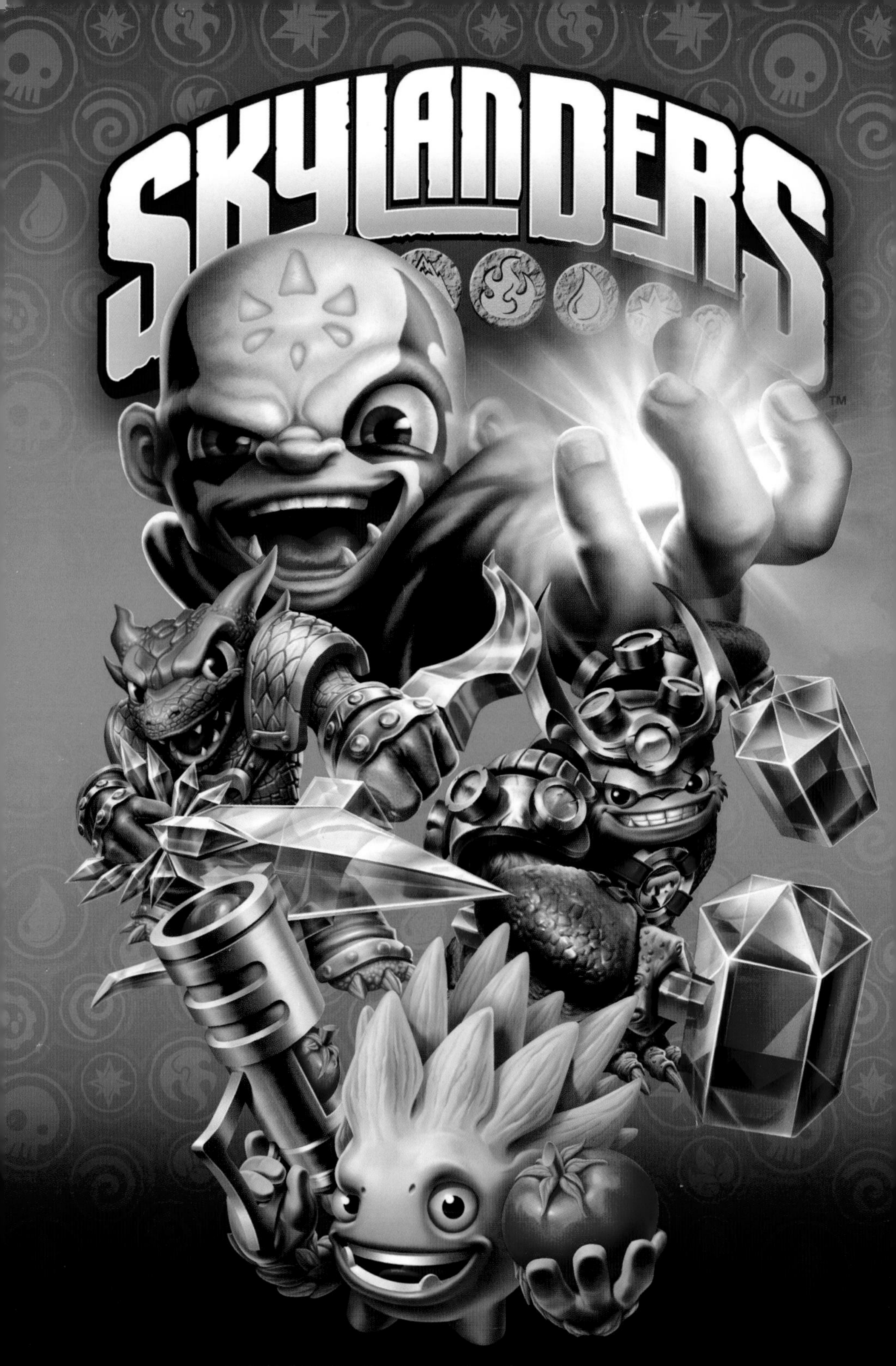
SKYLANDERS™

THE KAOS TRAP